Gold

Gold

John Wilson

ORCA BOOK PUBLISHERS

Library and Archives Canada Cataloguing in Publication

Wilson, John, author
Gold / John Wilson.
(Orca currents)

Issued in print and electronic formats.
ISBN 978-1-4598-1481-3 (softcover).—ISBN 978-1-4598-1482-0 (pdf).—
ISBN 978-1-4598-1483-7 (epub)

I. Title. II. Series: Orca currents
PS8595.I5834G665 2017   jc813'.54   c2017-900852-8
c2017-900853-6

First published in the United States, 2017
Library of Congress Control Number: 2017933018

Summary: In this high-interest novel for middle readers, Sam and Annabel
are on vacation in Italy and discover a hidden stash of gold.

*Orca Book Publishers is dedicated to preserving the environment and has
printed this book on Forest Stewardship Council® certified paper.*

Orca Book Publishers gratefully acknowledges the support for its
publishing programs provided by the following agencies: the Government
of Canada through the Canada Book Fund and the Canada Council for the
Arts,and the Province of British Columbia through the BC Arts Council
and the Book Publishing Tax Credit.

Edited by Tanya Trafford
Cover photography by iStock.com
Author photo by Katherine Gordon

ORCA BOOK PUBLISHERS
www.orcabook.com

Printed and bound in Canada.

20   19   18   17   •   4   3   2   1

For Caroline, with thanks for introducing me to Civita di Bagnoregio

Chapter One

"Foe
I have.
A crook collector
Of relics, books and bones.
Visiting Humphrey's mansion—
Discovers Sam in ice.
Recovers from clutch of
Battle Ford."

"What?" I ask.

Annabel and I are sitting at an outdoor café in the main square in Orvieto, Italy. I've been staring in awe at the ornate entrance to the city's cathedral while Annabel scribbles on the back of a napkin. "It's a piem," she says, as if that's supposed to mean something to me.

"Don't you mean a poem?"

"A piem is a poem written in Pilish."

Annabel has told me about Pilish, so this gives me a clue. "You mean the language where the number of letters in each word matches the numbers of Pi?"

"Exactly." Annabel puts on a wicked smile and goes on. "The language that Greg and I shared when we visited your mom in Canada."

Annabel hasn't stopped teasing me ever since we visited the dinosaur dig in Alberta. I'd gotten upset that this guy, who knew almost as much about the number Pi as she did, was hitting on her.

"You're never going to let me forget that, are you?"

"I think it's cute that you were jealous," she says. Her smile broadens. "And a little bit dumb that you thought I would dump you for someone like Greg."

"Okay," I say. "Enough about him. Let's see your piem."

Annabel turns her napkin around so I can read what she's written. I don't know Pi to thousands of numbers like she does, but I've learned enough to know that the number of letters in the words of her piem are the same as the beginning of Pi—3.14159265358979323846264...

"Very clever," I agree, "but it just goes to show how weird you are."

"But you've always known about my small obsession with Pi."

"Two things," I say. "One, it's *not* a small obsession, and two, we're sitting in the sun in Italy, across the square from a seven-hundred-year-old building that's one of the coolest things I've ever seen, and you are doodling. And what's this bit about me in ice?"

"Nothing personal. I needed a three-letter word. Don't you think it'd be neat to visit one of Humphrey Battleford's mansions and see some of the unique things he's collected?"

"Stolen, you mean, but yes, it would be cool. However, I doubt that he'll invite us any time soon."

"Oh, I don't know. He seems to like us. He even said he enjoys matching wits with us. He did set up that Arctic cruise so we would be a part of his scheme."

"And we have outfoxed him so far," I say, "but that doesn't mean he won't win if there's ever a next time. He has unlimited money."

"But we have brains," Annabel points out with a smile. "Okay, I have most of them, but you do help a little bit."

"Thanks very much," I say. Then I point at the piem. "At least I'm smart enough to notice that you made a mistake. *Battleford* is one word."

"Poetic license. I broke it up into six and four so it would work." She looks up. "Here's Mom and Dad."

I can see Annabel's parents winding their way between tour groups and pairs of scruffy backpackers. Even in the crowd, they stand out. For a start, Annabel's dad, Jack, is even taller than she is, and towers above everyone. He's wearing his usual uniform— hiking boots, khaki cargo pants and shirt covered in bulging pockets, and a wide-brimmed, beat-up bush hat. His long face is never clean-shaven, unruly tufts of red hair stick out from beneath his hat, and his piercing blue eyes are continually on the move, taking in every detail of the world and people around him.

In contrast, his wife, Pam, is at least a foot shorter and is always neatly dressed. Her honey-blond hair is stylishly cut, and she's wearing a bright, flowery summer dress and carrying a new Italian-leather shoulder bag. She sees us, smiles, waves and heads over. Jack, gazing at the low sun painting the front of the cathedral a dramatic gold, stumbles into a busload of Japanese tourists.

"Hello, you two," Pam says as she glides between the tables, kisses us both on the cheek and sits down. She loops her bag over the back of the chair and looks out onto the square. Jack is untangling himself from the tourists, who keep trying to take selfies with him. "I don't know how he ever gets anywhere." Pam shakes her head and catches the attention of a waiter. As Jack finally stumbles to our table and slumps into a chair, Pam orders two coffees and two more colas for Annabel and me.

"Do anything exciting today?" Jack asks.

Annabel immediately starts telling him about the buildings and art we've seen. Jack, who teaches history, chips in with facts and questions. When they begin to discuss which sculptures on the front of the cathedral were done by the fourteenth-century architect Lorenzo Maitani, Pam and I look at each other and raise our eyebrows. This has happened before.

"So, Sam," Pam says, "I think Maitani's very overrated. Don't you agree?"

"No. I think he's easily the best central defender the Italian soccer team's ever had."

Pam laughs out loud, Jack almost chokes on his coffee, and Annabel punches me on the arm.

"But seriously, Sam," Pam says. "What was *your* best part of today?"

"The caves and tunnels," I reply instantly. "The entire hill this town is built on is honeycombed with thousands of rooms and tunnels. Most are just wine and food storerooms under houses, but some of the tunnels and wells date back to the Etruscans thousands of years ago—even before the Roman empire."

"He kept wandering off," Annabel says. "The poor guide had to keep calling him back."

"It would be embarrassing," Pam says, "if we had to tell your parents that we'd lost you in a tunnel."

"But there must be tunnels under here that haven't been explored for centuries—maybe rooms filled with gold and silver," I say.

"I doubt it," Jack says. "People have been digging in the soft volcanic rock under this town for hundreds of years. It's very unlikely that you'll find any long-lost treasure." He winks at me.

I must look disappointed, because Jack quickly adds, "But there are lots of hill towns around here that are built on the same rock. I'm sure there are still things to be found. Are you still planning on going to Bagnoregio tomorrow?"

"Yeah," Annabel replies. "The buses are pretty good, so I think we'll set off early. Are you sure you don't want to come?"

"We'd love to," Pam replies, "but Jack still has some research in the archives, and I have to do some shopping for gifts to take home before we head back to Rome. So you two go off and have fun, and we'll meet up for a nice dinner tomorrow evening."

"Are there tunnels under Bagnoregio?" I ask.

"Yes," Jack says. "It's built on the same soft rock as Orvieto. But you'll need to be quick if you want to discover anything."

"What do you mean?" I ask.

"The rock's so soft that the hill the old town is built on is eroding. Every year it gets smaller as pieces slide into the surrounding valleys. Most of the population moved into the new town more than three hundred years ago."

"Cheap place to buy property," I suggest.

"Perhaps," Jack agrees, "but not a solid long-term investment."

Chapter Two

The local bus drops us off in Bagnoregio before any tourists arrive, so the only people around are locals out buying bread or sipping coffee at outdoor tables. "It was great of your parents to invite me along on this trip," I say to Annabel as we stroll the cobblestone streets.

"Yeah," Annabel agrees. "I grew up going on Dad's research trips. That's why

I'm so interested in history. While he was in some dark, dusty basement archive, I could wander around museums, castles and cathedrals to my heart's content."

Our first view of the old town takes our breath away.

The fog is still lingering in the valley in front of us, and Old Bagnoregio seems to be floating magically on a swirling carpet of gray.

"Awesome!" Annabel gasps. I can't think of a better description. It almost seems as if we could walk over the clouds and climb into the narrow streets that disappear into the ancient town.

The long bridge connecting the old and the new towns is beginning to emerge from the thinning fog when set off. As we climb the slope, Annabel says, "I can see why hardly anyone still lives here permanently." She's leaning on the bridge railing, staring at a recent landslide. Several feet of a house hang dangerously over a dizzying drop into the valley below.

"It could go at any minute," I say. "Let's not go too close to the edge when we're wandering around."

We walk through a long arch. For the first hour we have the town to ourselves. We wander aimlessly through the narrow, cobbled streets, marveling at the worn outdoor steps, the rough wooden doors that look old enough to have had Roman soldiers walk through them, and the odd stone hoops where donkeys used to be tethered. Most of the buildings have pots of flowers outside or vines snaking over their walls, giving the impression that nature is taking over the town.

In the main square, we check out the church that occupies one whole side. It's nothing special compared to some of the churches we've seen in Rome— until I notice something in the chapel. "There's a body here," I hiss at Annabel.

She moves to my side, and we both stare at the glass coffin below the altar. The corpse is dressed in old church clothes and is lying on its side in an awkward position. It's got a full beard and looks incredibly well preserved. "It's a statue," Annabel says, but she doesn't sound totally convinced.

"Why would they put a statue in a glass coffin?"

"Maybe they originally had the real saint's body in there but had to replace it with a statue when he started to decompose. Or maybe it's a miracle."

"Either way, it's creepy," I say, turning to leave.

Outside in the sunshine, we sit at the bottom of the church steps, leaning against a couple of old broken pillars and snacking on granola bars. Tourists are beginning to trickle in.

"You see all sorts," Annabel comments, nodding at a couple of men dressed in motorcycle leathers. One of them is large, has a shaved head and looks like an extra from an action movie. The other is considerably shorter, really skinny and has slicked-back black hair and a matching goatee. "Those two don't look like students of Etruscan history."

"True," I agree, "but motorbikes on the winding mountain roads around here would be cool. Oh man, check it out." I point to the edge of the square where a group of loudly dressed, camera-carrying tourists are following a guide waving a pink umbrella. "Let's get out of here before it gets too busy."

We stand and pick up our back-packs. "Why does the square have a dirt surface?" I wonder out loud. "Everywhere else in town is paved."

"It's for the donkey races," someone behind me says.

I turn, scraping my backpack against the pillar. "Careful," says a man with a mop of white hair and the thickest glasses I've ever seen. "That pillar comes from a Roman temple, although it may in fact have been stolen from an earlier Etruscan one. It was certainly here many hundreds of years before this church was built."

I look at the simple gray stone. It looks old, but then, so does everything here. "Donkey races?" I say.

"Every June and September," he says with a broad smile. "The donkeys would slip on cobbles, so we keep it dirt."

"Makes sense," Annabel agrees. "Bagnoregio's a fascinating old town."

"Indeed it is," the man says. "But you are not really in Bagnoregio. Only the new town across the bridge is called that. We are in Civita, or Ratumna, to be more exact—that's what the Etruscans called it. The two towns used to be one, but a violent earthquake in 1695 destroyed almost half the town and split what was left into two. The bishop moved to the new town and left the rest of us here to slowly slide into the valley. We are known as the Dying Town."

"You live here all year round?" I ask, hoping to prevent Annabel and this stranger from starting up a long, boring information exchange.

"Yes. Not many of us left. About twenty people, one dog…and many cats," he adds, glancing at three mangy cats slinking along the church wall. "But forgive me—where are my manners? My name is Pietro. Pietro Albani. I run the museum here." He waves vaguely across the square.

"I'm Sam Butler," I say, "and this is Annabel Sturridge. Pleased to meet you."

We both shake Pietro's hand. "I didn't know there was a museum in Bagno…I mean, Civita," Annabel says.

"It is my…how do you say…something I do for fun in my spare time?"

"Hobby?" I suggest.

Pietro nods. "Yes, hobby! I have been collecting artifacts for many years. I am just on my way to open up. Would you like to be the first visitors of the day?"

"We would love to," Annabel says. We cross the square and approach a rickety door. Next to it is a grubby, barely readable metal plate that says *Civita di Bagnoregio museo di storia.*

Pietro delves deep into his coat pocket and produces a large key. With much clanking and turning, he unlocks the door and pushes it open. As soon as he steps inside, he reaches up and punches a long code into a keypad on the wall. "I have little of great value here," he explains, "but one must be careful these days."

The museum is a collection of small linked rooms. The walls of each room are lined with dark wooden, glass-topped cabinets. Where there is space, cabinets stand like islands in the middle. The carpet is threadbare, the walls need a coat of paint, and the cabinets are covered in a layer of dust. The first case I peer into is filled with fragments of pottery and a small metal duck.

"The Etruscans had a walled town here more than twenty-five hundred years ago," Pietro explains as we browse.

"Did the Etruscans dig tunnels under their town?" I ask, remembering the tour we took under Orvieto.

"Certainly," Pietro says. "They dug tunnels, wells, rooms and tombs."

"Can we see them?" I ask eagerly.

"Probably not."

"Probably?" Annabel asks from the far corner of the room.

"Many are lost," Pietro says. "What you see now is only a tiny part of what must have been a large Etruscan town. The rest has fallen into the valley over the centuries."

"There might be some left though?" I ask.

"Yes," Pietro agrees, "but it is very difficult to tell whether a particular tunnel was dug by Etruscans, Romans, medieval monks or just a merchant two hundred years ago looking for a cool place to store his olive oil."

"Is all this"—Annabel sweeps her arm—"collected from the caves below Civita?"

"Mostly from here and nearby. People know of my hobby and bring me odd things they find in their cellars. But not all of it is Etruscan." Pietro leads us through to an adjoining small room. "This is where I keep my odds and ends." He walks around the room, pointing things out. "A Roman coin from the time of Julius Caesar, a broken cup from the Middle Ages, part of a crucifix from a church that fell into the valley long ago. And…" Pietro points to a chipped porcelain doll's head. "This was probably dropped by a scared child who took refuge in the caves when the Americans bombed this area in 1944. History doesn't end. It keeps going until it gets to us. Now, I will show you my greatest treasure."

Chapter Three

Pietro leads us into yet another room. This one has the usual collection of dusty cabinets except for one wall, where the only thing in sight is a large framed photograph of the town floating on a sea of fog, just as we saw earlier.

"It's beautiful," I say.

"It's just a tourist shot," Pietro says with a wave of his hand. He steps forward and lifts the picture from the wall to reveal a small safe set into the stone. "Even with the alarm system, it is often better to hide some things."

Blocking his hands from view, Pietro spins the dial in the center of the safe back and forth. The door swings open and he reaches in to pull out a small tray covered with a green cloth. As if he's handling a dangerous explosive, Pietro carries the tray to the nearest cabinet and gently sets it down. He beckons us closer and lifts the cloth. Annabel and I gasp at the same time.

Sitting on a rich-purple bed of velvet are five of the most beautiful objects I have ever seen. Placed on the four corners of the tray are a gold earring in the shape of a roaring lion, a bracelet made of what looks like woven gold thread, a gold ring with a huge ruby set in it, and a tiny golden wreath of oak leaves and acorns.

These are spectacular, but what causes us to gasp is the large brooch in the middle. It is made up of smaller circles, each with a tiny, incredibly detailed picture of a face, a creature or a plant, picked out in gold spots or lines so fine it is almost impossible to make them out.

"That's unbelievable," Annabel says at last.

"Beautiful, aren't they?" Pietro says. "They were probably the treasured jewels of a high-born Etruscan lady. Two and half millennia old and they look as if she just took them off when she went to bed last night."

"How can you be sure they're that old?" I ask.

"They were apparently found in an Etruscan tomb, although I only have the finder's word for that. But I am inclined to believe it, as the Etruscans were the world's best gold workers and used techniques that were lost long ago. I doubt there is a goldsmith today who could make something like this," Pietro says, gently touching the piece in the center.

"Were these found under Civita?" I ask, my mind quickly filling with visions of stumbling into a cave full of shining gold jewelry.

"I'm afraid not," Pietro says with smile. "They were first discovered many years ago. The story is that they are from the tombs at Monterozzi, but who knows? That's the difficulty with tomb robbers—the things they find may show up on the open market, but without knowing where they came from, what they were buried with and even how they were buried, so much valuable data is lost."

"That's the trouble with the way Humphrey Battleford does things," Annabel comments.

"Ah, you know Signor Battleford?"

Annabel and I turn and stare at Pietro, who blinks at us through his thick glasses.

"We *have* met him," Annabel says cautiously. "How do you know him?"

"He is a neighbor. He has a villa down in the valley." Pietro indicates the gold jewelry. "For many years he has been asking me to sell him these."

Annabel and I stare at each other as Pietro carefully rewraps his treasure and places it back in his safe.

"Gold is immortal," Pietro says as he spins the safe's lock. "It cannot be destroyed. It does not rust and can be melted down and reused many times. The gold jewelry you buy today might have first been part of the treasure of King Solomon's temple or hung around the neck of some Celtic warrior chief.

"I do not think anyone will find any Etruscan gold beneath Civita, but there is a more recent gold story," Pietro continues, turning to face us. "During the Second World War, the Nazis carried out the greatest theft in history. They stole paintings, sculptures and archaeological treasures from every country they invaded. They wanted to turn Berlin into the artistic center of the world. When they began to lose the war, the value of what they had looted became important for other reasons."

"Money to help the Nazi leaders escape and hide," Annabel guesses.

"Exactly. Works of art were sold for gold to rich collectors, and the gold was melted down into bars of bullion. They also melted down the jewelry and coins that they stole from those who were sent to their deaths in the concentration camps."

"What does this have to do with Civita?" Annabel asks.

"During the war, the Gestapo chief of this region was a truly evil man called Max Brunner. He had a sharp, hooked nose, and that, in addition to his infamous cruelty, gave him the nickname 'The Eagle of Death.' In 1944, Brunner realized that the war was lost and set about preparing his escape. The story goes that he hid gold bars in tunnels beneath an Italian hilltop town. He planned to collect it and escape, but he was killed in a bombing raid before he could return."

"Why do people think Brunner hid the gold in Civita and not one of the other hill towns?" I ask.

"No one knows for certain, but there are stories of trucks arriving in Bagnoregio and of soldiers wheeling heavy carts at night over the bridge into Civita. Nothing more is known.

Either the story is a complete fairy tale or Max Brunner's gold is still hidden somewhere below us. If it is true, then one day there will be a heavy rainstorm and a golden landslide will fall into the valley below.

"Until that day, we must wait. And I am not as rich as Signor Battleford. I must work." Pietro guides us toward the museum door. "It has been a pleasure to meet you both. Enjoy the remainder of your visit to my dying town."

"Thank you for showing us your treasures," Annabel says.

"And sharing your stories," I add.

Pietro smiles broadly and shakes our hands. "Please come back. You will always be welcome in my humble museum."

As we step through the door, we hear a dog bark. "That must be Civita's only dog," I say.

"No," Pietro says. "Bella is a very small dog. She has a high-pitched bark. That sounded like a much larger dog. A tourist must have brought it in. *Arrivederci.*"

"*Arrivederci,*" Annabel and I say together as we set off along a narrow, cobbled street.

"I can't believe Pietro knows Battleford," I say as soon as we're out of earshot. "We can't escape him, even in a tiny place like this."

"What better place for him to have one of his villas than a quiet valley where only a few tourists come?" Annabel says.

"Well," I say, "despite your piem, I hope we don't run into him."

We continue to walk and soon find ourselves at the edge of the town. The actual edge. Cautiously we peek over the wall down into the valley below.

"It seems such a shame that a town with over twenty-five hundred years of history is doomed," Annabel says.

"There are some optimists," I comment, pointing to where someone has propped up the basement of his house with concrete pillars.

"He's only delaying the inevitable. See how the rock has been washed away from around the pillars? The corner of the house is already beginning to sag."

"Not a good place to hold a dance," I say. "I see what your dad meant when he said that buying property here isn't a long-term investment."

"Is that a path down there?" Annabel asks, leaning farther over the edge.

"I think so," I say, not wanting to lean out far enough to be certain.

"Do you want to see if we can find a way down to it?"

"Okay," I agree, relieved to see that Annabel doesn't mean climbing over the wall and scaling the vertical cliff.

As we turn back onto the main street, a black shape leaps out at us from the shadows.

Chapter Four

We both jump back, startled, as the large dog lunges forward. Annabel recovers fastest. "Hello, Percy," she says, reaching down to scratch the dog's head while his tail beats the air frantically.

"Percy?" I say. The dog runs to me at the sound of his name and slobbers all over my trouser leg. "It is…you are…

what are you doing here?" I stammer. Percy gets even more excited as I pat him and talk to him. I'm pleased to see the dog, but worried that his master must be close by. Sure enough, a plump, middle-aged man steps around the corner. He's dressed in an expensive three-piece suit and carries a wooden cane.

"Well, well," the man says as a smile spreads across his face. "This *is* a pleasant surprise."

"What are you up to?" I blurt out.

Humphrey Battleford's smile stays firmly in place. "Hello to you too, Sam. I know we've had a few run-ins in the past, but that doesn't mean I'm totally evil. I'm just a regular guy. Perhaps I have more money than most people, and that allows me to collect beautiful things, but who does not like to be surrounded by beauty? And I take better care of my collections than many museums do."

"You live nearby, don't you?" Annabel asks before I can say something else rude.

"I do," Battleford replies. "I have a modest house down in the valley. This is such a beautiful part of the world, and Percy does love the walks we take in the hills. I am simply here for a holiday, just as I suspect you two are. I love these old hilltop towns."

We're interrupted by a tour group pushing past us, forcing us to one side of the narrow street. They ignore us, chattering noisily and photographing randomly.

"However, I think it is time for me to move on to somewhere more quiet," Battleford says after they have passed. "It is hard to appreciate the past when the present"—he waves at the disappearing tourists—"is so invasive. How long are you staying in Civita?"

"We're just here for the day," Annabel says.

"Enough time to see the surface," Battleford says. "If you were staying longer, I would offer to show you the part of my collection I keep here. I am sure it would interest you. But perhaps I could buy you both lunch a little later. We do have one restaurant in town, and it serves a very nice dish of polenta and wild boar."

"No, thank you," I say abruptly. "We brought lunch."

Battleford nods. "And you don't wish to spend time with such a vicious criminal as myself. No matter. Maybe some other time. Do enjoy the rest of your day. Come along, Percy, we have imposed enough on these charming young people."

Battleford moves off and Percy reluctantly tears himself away from my attention and follows. Annabel and I stand and stare until both are out of sight.

"I can't believe he offered to buy us lunch," I say. "He has no shame."

"I don't think huge amounts of money and shame go together," Annabel says. "Still, lunch might have been interesting."

"After all we've been through and all he has tried to do, I can't believe you would have actually accepted his offer of lunch."

"You know what they say." Annabel threads her arm through mine, and we start walking again. "Know your enemy."

"Do you think he's here to steal something?" An idea jumps into my mind. "It would be easy for someone like

Battleford to steal Pietro's gold jewelry. His safe didn't look very big or fancy, and that Etruscan jewelry would probably look good in Battleford's collection."

"True," Annabel agrees, "but if he was going to steal Pietro's gold, why hasn't he done it by now? Pietro told us that Battleford has been trying to buy his jewelry for years."

"I suppose," I say. "And it's probably not a good idea for him to steal this close to one of his homes."

The road stops at what is left of a garden. A dirt track about five feet wide runs around the hillside to our right. "This looks as if it might lead to the path we saw from above," Annabel says.

"I hope it doesn't lead to the edge of another cliff," I say, but Annabel has already started down the track, and I have no choice but to follow.

As we descend, the cliff of coarse brownish rock looms on my right. Above me, buildings teeter dangerously. One has recently lost a section of its outside wall, and empty rooms gape like black mouths over the valley.

Beside the path, the entrance to a cave is blocked by a rough wooden fence and a homemade gate. "I'm going to have look in there," I say to Annabel, who's a few steps ahead of me.

"Okay," she says over her shoulder. "Shout if you need a hand to carry out all the gold." She continues around the corner.

"I'll catch up with you," I say with a laugh. I walk over and peer between the slats of the fence. It's dark, and it takes a few moments for my eyes to adjust. The cave is about the size of a single-car garage. The curved roof is carved out of the rough stone of the cliff.

Narrow shafts of sunlight cut through the dusty air and land on stacks of what look like gardening tools, pots of varying sizes, piles of rusting machinery and a brand-new red ATV.

Well, what do you know, I think with a smile, the Etruscans had ATVs.

"This is private property," says someone directly behind me.

I spin around to see the two motor-cycle guys we noticed earlier. The big one is standing on the path, and the skinny one is only a couple of feet away from me. "Sorry," I say, disturbed that I didn't hear either of them approach. "I was just wandering down the track and wanted to take a peek. I thought this cave might be full of Etruscan treasure."

My weak attempt at humor doesn't go down well. The skinny guy stares hard at me, his eyes narrow and dark. In a heavy accent he says, "Yeah, well, it is best that you not pry into the business of other people." He reaches into his pocket, and I have the sudden fear that he's reaching for a gun. But it turns out he's just after the key to the padlock on the gate.

"Sorry," I say again and move back onto the track. The big guy glares at me unpleasantly. I nod and smile but get no reaction. I force myself not to run but walk very quickly to catch up with Annabel.

"I just met those motorcycle guys we saw in town," I say as I reach her. "They're definitely not Etruscan historians. The skinny guy said I was on private property. He had an accent, German, I think, and they were both kind of creepy."

Annabel looks concerned. "Do you think the cave belonged to them?"

"Yes," I reply, beginning to relax now that I am back in familiar company. "They had a key to the gate. The place was full of tools and an ATV."

"So they're not tourists. I wonder…?"

"What?"

"I'm not sure. They're not Italian, they're not tourists, and they own, or at least rent, something around here. Do we know anyone else who fits that description?"

"Humphrey Battleford. Do you think they work for him?"

"I don't know, but we do know that Battleford often hires people to do his dirty work for him. And don't forget what Pietro said."

"I thought we'd decided that Battleford would have stolen Pietro's Etruscan gold by now if he was going to."

"The Etruscan gold, yes, but Pietro told us about other gold that might be here."

"The Nazi gold that the Gestapo officer hid."

"Max Brunner," Annabel says. "If anyone has the resources to find Brunner's hidden gold, it would be Battleford."

"And finding Nazi gold wouldn't be like stealing from his neighbors. Can we never escape Battleford?"

Chapter Five

As we descend, we are treated to spectacular views out over the valley below. Single-track roads snake back and forth through the trees and between sharp hills of eroded gray rock. Scattered farms are surrounded by the regular patterns of olive trees or grapevines. A large stone building with a round tower rising from one end stands on a low hill above a small village.

We walk around another corner and come to a fork in the track. Straight ahead it continues as a narrow, over-grown path that twists steeply down the hillside. To the right a wider track disap-pears into a dark hole in the cliff. There is an official-looking strip of yellow plastic tape strung between two rough posts at the entrance.

"I don't think they want us to go any farther," Annabel says. But she goes right up to the tape, leans over and peers into the hole. "It's a tunnel. It must go right through the hill. I can see light at the other end."

I stand beside her. The tunnel is wide and high enough for several people to walk side by side. It's dark for a short stretch in the middle, but then it brightens with light from the other end. It looks safe.

"There's probably a path at the other end that will take us back up to Civita," Annabel suggests.

"They've taped it off for a reason," I say. I don't want to be caught doing something wrong in a country where we don't even speak the language.

"It looks fine," Annabel says, ducking under the tape. "There are no cave-ins, and look, there's garbage. People have been in here recently. Come on."

Reluctantly I follow Annabel as she moves farther into the tunnel. She's right—the ground is hard-packed earth, and the rock walls and roof appear solid. There are several small caves off the tunnel on both sides. Peering into the blackness tells us nothing. The caves could be either a couple of feet deep or lead into an endless labyrinth of tunnels and rooms.

"I wish we had a flashlight," Annabel says.

I don't. It was one thing to wander the tunnels below Orvieto with electric lights and a cheerful guide who kept counting us to make sure no one got lost. Even the lure of Etruscan gold doesn't make crawling into the unknown blackness with just a flashlight attractive.

Our explorations are interrupted by the sound of an engine outside the tunnel. "That sounds like an ATV," I say. The noise of the engine dies and is replaced by voices. Two figures appear silhouetted in the light, one tall and bulky, the other shorter and skinny. Although we probably can't be seen in the shadows of the tunnel, we both instinctively step back into the darkness.

"We must search every cave." I recognize the voice of the skinny guy. "We shall begin at the far end and work our way back."

Annabel finds my hand in the dark and squeezes it. She must be as nervous as I am.

The voices get louder as the men advance along the tunnel. The skinny one seems to be doing all the talking. "We search for the eagle looking to its left. The clues in my grandfather's diary pointed us this way, and he was the one who knew. We are at the correct place. I expect that much digging will be required, but when we find the eagle that Grandfather carved, we will know we are close."

I hold my breath as they pass. Their footsteps sound loud in the confined space, and the narrow beams of two flashlights sweep the floor. The skinny guy is still talking. "He said the gold was deep in the hillside. This is the deepest part, so this is where we must begin."

"Looks like it's a popular spot," says the other guy. I'm surprised by his

American accent. "Party time on Saturday night." I hear the sound of an empty can being kicked along the ground. "We ain't about to find anything here, Kurt, and I hate going on wild-goose chases."

"Have some faith, Ethan. We do not chase wild gooses. The eagle is here somewhere."

The footfalls fade as the pair moves along the tunnel, and I let out my breath. I pluck up the courage to peer out. I can see them walking along each side of the tunnel. Whenever they pass a cave, they shine their powerful flashlights inside.

"They're going to find us," I say, drawing back into the cave. I'm not sure why I'm so scared. They're just a couple of guys looking for some kind of eagle. Okay, they're a bit creepy and might be working for Humphrey Battleford, but that doesn't mean we're in any danger. Yet I *am* scared. "We should get out."

"Yes," Annabel agrees. "Walk out casually."

Before I have time to wonder if this is a good idea, Annabel, still holding my hand, steps out into the tunnel. Side by side, we walk toward the entrance.

At first we're in the darkest part of the tunnel, but as we get closer to the light of day, we become more visible. My breathing is shallow, and I'm sweating way too much. Annabel is holding my hand in a viselike grip. But we're getting close. Looks like we're going to make it.

"Hey!" It's the skinny one, Kurt. "You two. Stop! You shouldn't be in here. Come here right now!" The sound of running feet echoes down the tunnel.

If you hear footsteps behind you getting closer, it's impossible not to run. That's exactly what Annabel and I do— we drop hands and run as fast as we can.

We burst out into the sunshine and almost collide with the ATV. It's parked at an angle, blocking the path we came down. "This way," I say, turning and heading for the overgrown path leading down the hillside. As I turn, I glance back at the tunnel. The big one called Ethan is leading the way, but Kurt is close behind. They both look angry.

With Annabel right behind me, I charge along the path, branches slapping at my face and legs. The path's rough and getting steeper. I'm running too fast, but there's so much adrenaline pumping through me that I can't stop. At least Ethan and Kurt can't follow us in the ATV. I'm pretty sure we can keep ahead of them until we can find a way back up to the town.

My next step is into open air. I yell as my body spins out of control. I land painfully on my side and begin sliding down the steep slope in a shower of dirt and small rocks. From somewhere far above, I can hear Annabel screaming my name.

Chapter Six

I feel dizzy, and my head hurts. I'm lying on my back, and all I can see are a few puffy white clouds drifting across the expanse of blue sky. It's peaceful. Maybe I can just lie here and relax. A steadily increasing ache in my left leg distracts me, pulling me away from the beautiful sky. I gradually become aware of my entire body. It feels scraped and bruised, and I'm covered in dust. The ache in my leg is becoming a sharp pain. The leg is bent under me, and my knee is wedged against a large rock. I'm going to have to do something to relieve the pressure.

I try to sit up and grunt at the pain as the movement puts more pressure on my bent leg. I lie back and dig my elbows into the slope, trying to work my body up the slope. My efforts trigger small avalanches of stones and dirt that trickle past me. The pressure on my left knee eases, and I'm able to swing my good right leg over and push against the rock. The rock moves slightly, and I inch myself far enough up the slope that I can unbend my left leg. It hurts, but the sense of relief overwhelms the pain.

I carefully move my leg. It's not broken. I breathe a sigh of relief and sit up. Then I see something that sets my heart racing and chills the sweat on my body.

Less than a foot past the rock I've been pushing against, the slope I slid down ends—in nothing. I am right on the edge of a cliff. The pebbles my movements have dislodged bounce down and disappear in the void. They could be falling a few feet or a hundred feet. I swallow hard as I think what would have happened if the rock hadn't stopped my slide or if my efforts to free my leg had started the rock moving. Like those pebbles, I'd be at the bottom of the cliff, either dead or severely injured.

I sit very still, focusing on controlling my ragged breathing. Once I've calmed down a bit, I look around.

The slope I've come down is the result of a recent landslide. A wide swath of rocks, dirt and broken branches, it's too steep and unstable to climb. One edge of the slide is quite far away, and the thought of trying to crawl across the slope with the deadly drop right beside me almost brings on a panic attack. The other edge is only a couple of feet away from me. I can reach over and touch it, but there's nothing to hold on to. I need something to grab. A handful of dirt or grass won't help me as I plummet over the cliff.

Turning my head, I see a small tree, behind me and slightly upslope. A root is sticking out of the bank. If I can reach it, and if the tree is still firmly anchored, I should be able to haul myself out of the slide and away from the cliff.

Very slowly, and trying not to put any pressure on the rock, I lie back down. I stretch my left arm back above my head and grope for the root. I can feel it with my fingertips, but no matter how hard I stretch, I can't quite grip it. I have to move up the slope.

Slowly I pull my feet away from the rock. I carefully dig my heels into the loose dirt and push. The rock tilts slightly, so I stop.

I move my feet up until my knees are bent as far as they will go. My left knee is killing me, but I ignore the pain. I try to push myself higher up the slope. My heels dig in, but my feet slip down. Slow and careful isn't going to work. I am going to have to lunge. Again I pull my feet up as far as I can. I plan my movements, take a deep breath and shove.

My feet slip down but my body moves up. I grab the root with my left hand, praying that it won't come loose or break away. Then I quickly roll over and grab the root with my right hand. Now I have a good grip on the root with both hands. I hear a noise below me and twist my head in time to see the rock that saved my life disappearing over the edge. It feels like a very long time before I hear the rock crash into the valley below.

Scrambling with my feet and pulling with my arms, I drag myself up until I can get my feet onto the root. Without stopping, I hurl myself off the root and onto the bank. I collect some new cuts and scrapes, but the feeling of being on stable ground again is wonderful. I crawl away from the landslide until I reach a decent-sized tree. I sit with my back to the trunk and begin to shake.

At last my mind lets go of the images of my broken body twisting through space over the cliff edge, and I start thinking about what to do next. And where is Annabel?

I heard her scream when I fell, but nothing since. Surely I couldn't have fallen so far that she's out of earshot. Why is she not calling for me?

"Annabel!" I yell as loudly as I can.

Nothing.

I call out a few more times, listening for the faintest sound from above.

Nothing.

Now I'm worried. Has she already gone to get help, or did those creeps grab her? I need to get back up there. Carefully, and favoring my sore leg as much as possible, I begin to work my way up the steep slope. The ground is firm, and there are bushes and small trees I can use to pull myself up, but it's hard work, and even my good right knee begins to hurt after a while. I make progress, stopping every few minutes to shout Annabel's name. The longer I go without hearing any response, the more worried I become. What has happened to her?

Chapter Seven

I finally reach the overgrown path and work my way back to where I went over the edge. There's no sign of Annabel. I call out her name once more without much hope of a reply. She *must* have gone for help. Perhaps Ethan and Kurt aren't as creepy as I thought. Maybe they caught up to her and she persuaded them to take her to the town to get help.

If that's the case, someone will be along soon to find me. I should wait here so I don't miss them and become really lost. I do vaguely wonder why at least one of them didn't stay here to look for me or wait to see if I managed to scramble back up the slope.

I check my body for damage. Mostly it's scratches and scrapes. They sting, but there's not much blood. I have a lump on the back of my head and several other places where I'll bruise for sure. My left knee still hurts, but overall I don't think I've sustained any serious damage.

Holding tightly onto a branch, I lean out and look down the slide. It stretches a long way, and I can see the top of the cliff. The place where the rock stopped my fall is hidden behind vegetation. That would explain why Annabel went for help immediately. If she didn't actually see my fall, a quick glance would have convinced her that

I had disappeared over the cliff. I feel like throwing up when I think of how close I came to a horrible death—and how worried Annabel must be.

I twist around and look up the slope. The landslide exposed a large oval of fresh rock beneath the town. It looks as if someone has taken a giant spoon, scooped a hole in the hillside and dumped it down the slope. In the middle of the scoop, and probably the reason the slope was so weak here, there is a dark hole—a newly exposed cave.

There's a lot of dirt and rubble around the cave entrance, but the rocks on either side look too regular to be natural. I feel a pulse of excitement. Could this be an undiscovered Etruscan tomb? It's probably just someone's abandoned wine cellar, but…

I look around. It wouldn't take long to scramble up and check it out. I can stay beside the landslide, so I won't be in any danger of falling, and I will still be close enough to hear if a rescue party shows up. I begin to climb.

Within minutes I'm beside the scoop. I'm right about the cave— the entrance has been carved out of the rock. The base of the scoop forms quite a wide ledge that leads to the cave. It's secure, but I still don't look down as I edge along.

Peering into the darkness from the bright sunlight, I can't make out a thing. But something on the step into the cave catches my eye. It's a crude carving cut deeply into the soft rock. It seems to be a bird with outstretched wings. Its head is turned to the left. It's the bird that Ethan and Kurt were looking for! But what does it mean? Kurt said something about digging deep for gold. Etruscan gold?

I step into the mouth of the cave and stare hard into the darkness. Gradually my eyes adjust and I begin to see more.

I take a few careful steps. The cave is actually a square room. The flat ceiling is just above my head, and the walls just wider than I can stretch out my arms. I can't see how far back it goes, so I move forward.

The floor is thick with dust, and my shuffling steps stir it up, irritating my nose. Feeling my way along the left-hand wall, I make out a shape in the gloom, an old, rotting wooden chest. The front and one side of the chest have completely collapsed, and whatever was in the chest has slumped into a dust-covered pile on the floor.

I step forward and stub my toe on a rock, jarring my sore knee. I look down. The rock looks more like a small brick. I bend over and pick it up. It's heavy, way heavier than a brick of that size should be. And an odd shape for a brick, come to think of it. I take it back out to the cave entrance and wipe the dirt off.

I can feel marks on it, writing or some sort of logo. When it's cleaner and I can see it properly, I almost drop it down the slope. It's not a brick—it's a gold bar.

I crouch down and spit on the bar, wiping it as clean as I can. The first shape I make out is an eagle like the one carved on the rock, but much neater. This one is standing on a circle enclosing the Nazi swastika.

Below the eagle are the words *Deutsche Reichsbank, 1 Kilo Feingold, 999.9*. There is a series of letters and numbers below that. My mind races back to the story Pietro told us—I haven't found an Etruscan tomb filled with gold jewelry. I've stumbled on Max Brunner's looted Nazi gold! Is that why Humphrey Battleford is here in Civita? Has he hired Kurt and Ethan to find the gold for him?

All of a sudden, the idea that Kurt and Ethan might be helping Annabel vanishes.

Those two aren't just any treasure hunters. They're Battleford's men, searching for Nazi gold. Battleford has mostly been polite with us, but that has always been when he thought he had won and gotten what he wanted. The one time he hadn't been polite was in Australia, when he thought I could stop him from getting what he wanted, and he had threatened me with a pistol. Would he have used it? I certainly thought so at the time. Would he hire a couple of sketchy characters like Kurt and Ethan? No doubt about it.

So Annabel sees me disappear down the slope and screams. Kurt and Ethan arrive. They look down the slide and think I've gone over the edge to my death. The last thing they would want is the police and the authorities crawling all over the hillside where they think the gold is. So they grab Annabel and take her with them. But where to?

To Humphrey Battleford? It seems unlikely. The last thing Battleford wants is to be directly involved in the illegal activities his hirelings get up to.

Kurt and Ethan must have panicked and decided to hide Annabel until they could finish their search for the eagle and the gold. That would explain why Annabel didn't come looking for me. But where would they have taken her?

I am standing in the sunshine, right next to a cave full of stolen gold, sweat prickling my sides. I feel totally helpless. The shock of almost dying and then figuring out that Annabel has probably been kidnapped by Battleford's men is almost more than I can take. In all our fights with Battleford, Annabel and I have always been together. When one of us feels down, the other encourages. When one of us sees no way forward, the other comes up with an idea. I freely admit that Annabel has come up with most of the best ideas, but we're still a team. Now I'm on my own. It's all up to me.

I close my eyes, clench my fists and struggle to regain control. Standing here crying won't do me any good. Help isn't going to magically arrive. I have to do something. I look around. If I'm going to move, there's only one way to go. I take a deep breath, slide the gold bar into my pocket, scramble down the hillside to the overgrown path and head back up the hill. "I'm coming, Annabel," I say under my breath.

Chapter Eight

As I walk, I try to think of a plan. Obviously, I should try and find Annabel, but where do I start? My only option is to check everywhere as I go along.

At the tunnel entrance, there's no sign of the ATV. I peer in and let my eyes adjust to the gloom. It looks empty. The yellow plastic tape is still in place, and it doesn't allow room for an ATV to go under or around it. Of course, they could have stored the ATV back in the cave.

The wooden gates are closed and padlocked. I peer in—no ATV. So Kurt and Ethan must have taken the ATV, and Annabel, up the hill into Civita. That's where I have to go next, but what will I do when I get there? I doubt if a dying town of twenty people has a police station. If there is one, it'll be over in Bagnoregio, and that's a long walk back. All I can think to do is seek out Pietro, the only person I know in the town, and ask for his help. Slowly, my knee complaining with every step and the gold weighing heavily in my pocket, I slog up the hill into town.

I'm exhausted, aching and drenched in sweat by the time I reach the crowded main square. With a silent prayer that Pietro hasn't locked up and gone home,

I knock on the museum door. Eventually, the door opens and Pietro peers out.

"It is you," he says. "I did not expect you back so soon." Pietro runs his eyes over me. "And you do not look too good. What happened?" He glances over my shoulder. "And where is your charming friend?"

"I had an accident," I explain. "I need help."

Pietro hesitates, which I find odd since he was so keen earlier to invite us in and show us his treasures. He glances back into the room behind him before he opens the door wider. "You had better come in and tell me what happened."

I enter the room, and Pietro drags a chair out of the corner and invites me to sit. The number of tourists in the square seems to have no effect on how many visit the museum. The place is as deserted as it was when we first came in.

I give Pietro the short version. I tell him about my fall, my lucky escape and my struggle back up the hill. I say that we saw a couple of shady characters and that they and Annabel were missing when I climbed back up to the path. Then I hesitate, unsure whether to tell Pietro that I suspect Battleford may be involved.

Pietro, assuming I've finished my story, says, "They probably went to find help."

"Why didn't one of them stay and look for me?"

Pietro stares hard at me for a minute. "The place you fell is very dangerous. There are many rockfalls along there, and they all end in that cliff you almost went over. You are extremely lucky to be alive. If those men knew the area, they would reasonably assume that you were dead. They probably did not want to leave your young friend alone in case she tried to find you and fell to her death herself."

"It was impossible to see where I landed," I agree, "but I don't think the two men were locals. One had a German accent, and the other was American."

"Still…" Pietro says uncertainly. "They may have gone over to Bagnoregio to inform the police of the tragedy."

"They came up the hill in a red ATV," I point out. "The only way to reach the bridge over to Bagnoregio is through the square outside. Did you hear an ATV go past?"

"No," Pietro says. His brow creases. "And there is no place to hide an ATV between where you came up the track and the square."

"So where could they have gone?"

I hear a familiar voice coming from the next room. "As my great fellow

American Thomas Alva Edison once said, *When you have exhausted all possibilities, remember this—you haven't.*"

Despite my aching body, I jump to my feet and gape over Pietro's shoulder. Humphrey Battleford is standing in the doorway, a quiet smile on his face.

I push past Pietro and stand toe-to-toe with Battleford. I'm a couple of inches taller than he is, which makes me feel powerful. "What are you doing here?" I yell in his face. "What have you done with Annabel?"

My shouting has no apparent effect. His smile doesn't even flicker. "I don't believe I have done anything with your delightful companion," he says calmly.

"Your thugs have kidnapped her. Where have they taken her?"

"My dear Sam. I admit that sometimes circumstances force me to employ some helpers who are, how shall we say, not of the finest quality. But thugs? I would never stoop that low, and as for kidnapping, goodness me, I had hoped that by now you would think better of me than that."

"Your men, Kurt and Ethan, took her from the hillside after I fell. I call that kidnapping." My voice is quieter now. It's hard to keep yelling at someone if the yelling has no effect.

"I am glad to see that you are calmer now, Sam. Please believe that I have neither a Kurt nor an Ethan in my employ, and that I would never dream of putting you or Annabel in any danger."

I've calmed down enough by now not to mention the time Battleford pointed a gun at me or abandoned Annabel and me on a remote Arctic island. It wouldn't do any good. And anyway, I'm beginning to believe him.

"If you don't employ Kurt and Ethan, then who do they work for?"

"A good question, Sam. Perhaps they work for themselves. In any case, I have a feeling you haven't told us everything that happened on the hillside. Why don't you sit back down and fill in the blanks?"

I sit back down. I describe Kurt and Ethan, how they scared us in the tunnel and then chased us along the path. I don't want to tell Battleford about finding the cave with the carved eagle and the gold, but I don't see that I have a choice. I need help. Whether Battleford kidnapped Annabel or not, maybe telling him about the gold is the only way to get his help.

"There's a cave at the top of the landslip," I say. "It has a human-made entrance with an eagle carved on it, and inside there's a box of these." I pull the gold bar out of my pocket and hold it out.

Behind me Pietro gasps. "So the stories are true!"

"It would appear so," Battleford says, reaching out and lifting the gold bar from my hand. I let him take it. He turns it over slowly. "Gold," he says thoughtfully. "Throughout history men have done incalculable evil to obtain it. But who is after this store?"

We all three stare at the gold in silence. Then something I forgot to mention pops into my head. "When I overheard Kurt in the tunnel, he told Ethan that it was his grandfather who had carved the eagle in the rock. He also said his grandfather had kept a diary with clues that had led him here. Does that mean that Kurt's grandfather was here during the war?"

"It's certainly possible," Battleford says. "He would have been the right age to have been a soldier in the war against the Nazis." Battleford turns the gold bar over in his hand and looks up at me. "If Kurt's grandfather was here during the war and hid the gold in the cave, why didn't he come back and collect it?"

Battleford tilts his head to one side, encouraging me to answer.

Suddenly it's all clear. "Because he was killed in a bombing raid," I say.

Battleford smiles and nods. "But he wrote clues in his diary that would one day lead someone in his family to the treasure? Kurt's grandfather was Max Brunner."

Behind me I hear Pietro utter a soft whisper, "The Eagle of Death."

Chapter Nine

The room suddenly feels very cold. I was angry at Battleford when I thought Kurt and Ethan worked for him, but deep down I didn't believe that Annabel was in any serious danger. Now that I know Kurt is the grandson of a ruthless Nazi, I'm terrified that Annabel could be in real danger.

"Annabel," I say, turning to the door. "I have to go and look for her."

"And where do you plan to begin your search?" says Battleford calmly. He is beginning to get on my nerves.

"I don't know," I say, "but I have to do something." I'm panicky, but Battleford's question has stopped me from rushing out the door. I have no idea where to start.

"Think it through before you run off with all guns firing. You know that these guys took Annabel away in the red ATV and that they did not come through town. Neither Pietro nor I heard them pass."

"Then where did they go?" I ask.

"There's a track at the other end of the tunnel that leads down into the valley. I use it myself sometimes when I come up to town."

"But the tape hadn't been moved." Even as I say this, I realize my mistake.

"Yellow plastic tape is easy enough to replace," Battleford points out.

"So they took Annabel down into the valley. We have to go and rescue her." I take another step toward the door.

"I shall make some phone calls," Battleford says.

"It'll take forever to convince the police to do something and for them to get organized. Annabel's in trouble now. I'm going to find her."

"And nothing I can say will change your mind?"

"No," I say.

"Then I suppose I could restrain you." Battleford looks at me. I glance toward the door. Pietro has quietly moved and is now blocking my escape route. "But I did tell you that kidnapping was not something I indulged in," Battleford goes on, a smile creasing his pudgy face. "I suppose the only alternative left to me is to offer you what assistance I can. Pietro, would you be prepared to lend your old bicycle to our young friend?"

"But of course," Pietro replies. He steps past me. "Please come this way." He leads us through the museum and out onto a small, shaded patio. Percy is tied up at one side and goes berserk when he sees us. Beside him, propped up against the wall, is a red bicycle that has seen better days.

"It is not the peak of modern mountain-bike technology," Battleford says, "but the track down the mountain is not too rough, and, if you take care, it will take you down faster than walking."

"Thank you," I say.

Pietro steps forward and lifts the bike away from the wall. "It is aged but solid. It is fixed-gear," he adds. "You know this type of bicycle?"

"I know it, but I've never ridden one."

"You cannot, how do you say, run free?"

"Freewheel," I say.

"Exactly," Pietro says. "The pedals are fixed so that they must always turn. You can use them to stop too much speed on the hillside better than the brakes."

"I'll manage," I say. I'm not certain I can, but I'm prepared to try if it saves me time.

"Once in the valley, you will see several farms and old ruined buildings," Battleford tells me. "I think it's likely they will have taken Annabel to one of them. I suggest you look around carefully, and if you see the ATV, call me. You have a cell phone?"

I take my iPhone out, and Battleford gives me his number to program in. "Tell me where you are and I will send help. I really would not recommend attempting to tackle these men on your own." Battleford looks at me seriously. "Will you promise me that?"

"I will be careful," I say.

Battleford nods and unties Percy. "Take Percy with you. Despite appearances, he is a clever dog. He will follow you and do as he is told."

I'm not keen on the idea of taking Percy. He's a nice dog, but I can't see what use he'll be. However, I'm eager to be off and don't want to stand here arguing. "Thanks," I say and wheel the bike out into the tiny lane behind the patio. I forget that the pedals will turn when the back wheel does, and one cracks me painfully on the ankle bone.

"Be careful," Pietro advises.

"I will make some calls and wait for yours," Battleford says. "Help will be with you soon."

Standing well clear of the pedals, I push the bike along the alley onto the slightly wider street that leads back to the town square. Percy trots at my side. "Good dog," I say, and he wags his tail.

I pedal slowly through the streets, getting used to the fixed gear and avoiding the wandering tourists. I think how strange it feels to have Battleford on my side, helping me rescue Annabel.

Thoughts of Annabel bring back my worry. What will I find at the bottom of the hill? How quickly will Battleford get the police to respond when I call—assuming that I spot the ATV and find Annabel?

Percy and I soon reach the tunnel. I hesitate at the tape, but Percy simply runs under it as if leading the way. I push through the tape and don't bother to replace it. At the other end of the tunnel the track is much steeper. "Hang in there, Annabel! I'm coming to get you!" I cry, launching myself down the mountainside.

Chapter Ten

Trying to control the speed of the unfamiliar bike down the steep slope, especially approaching sudden sharp corners, is a nightmare. The brakes do little more than slow me gently, so I have to learn to control my speed by slowing the pedals. Sometimes I overdo it and the rear wheel locks, sending me skidding in a cloud of dust toward the cliff edge.

Percy seems to know the way and often rushes on ahead, but he always returns to see how I'm doing. I'm glad to still be alive when the slope eventually eases and the track improves and straightens out. Percy takes up a position beside me.

For a while I cycle through trees and have a chance to catch my breath and slow my heart rate. My knees, which have no chance of resting on a fixed-gear bike, hurt, but thoughts of Annabel keep me going.

I stop on top of a small hill and look around. Percy is beside me, his tongue flopping out of the side of his mouth. "So what do we do now?" I ask him. Percy's tail thumps on the ground in reply.

I'm looking down over neatly divided areas of olive groves, the trees planted in precise, straight lines.

Each grove has a large farmhouse and a collection of outbuildings at its center. In the distance I can see the large stone building and tower that we noticed from Civita.

"I can see eight farms," I tell Percy. "Trouble is, they're all a long way off the main road. If the bad guys are hiding out in one of them, I'll be pedaling right into their arms. I need a plan, Percy. Any ideas?"

Percy doesn't reply. "Okay then," I say. "First, let's assume that Kurt and Ethan want to stay close to the gold, so they are nearby." Percy thumps his tail. "Second, neither of them is a local, so they're probably not living on one of the well-established farms. If I were them, I'd rent a place, probably somewhere as isolated as possible. So we ignore the big farms and look for someplace that looks like it could be rented. What do you think?"

Percy looks at me and tilts his head to one side. "Okay, it's not much of a plan, but do you have anything better?" Percy licks his lips. "I thought not. Now let's get moving and rescue Annabel." With a grunt at the renewed pain in my knees and with Percy at my side, I push off down the hill.

I'm in pain, worried sick about Annabel and with no clear idea of what I'm doing or getting into. The one thing I'm happy about is Battleford suggesting that I bring Percy. His loyalty is simple, and talking to him helps me clear my thoughts.

The first few turnoffs we pass have signs that read *Strada Privata*, which my very limited Italian and guesswork tell me means "private road." Then I see a sign that I pull over to read more carefully—*Agriturismo Civita*. *Turismo* must mean "tourist." Is this a holiday farm for rent?

"Let's check this one out," I say to Percy as I pedal slowly up the winding road between rows of grapevines. Ahead of me I can see a huge mansion with a pillared entrance. It's surrounded by a high metal fence. The gates are locked, but I peer through at the immaculate lawn, scattered statues and the corner of what must be a very large swimming pool. I doubt very much if Kurt and Ethan would be staying at a place like this.

Before I have a chance to retreat, a middle-aged man on a riding lawn mower appears around the corner of the garage. He sees me and heads over. Percy growls quietly. The man dismounts and looks at Percy and me with disdain. We're clearly not the sort of tourists who would stay at a place like this—I look pretty beat-up and neither of us is very clean. I silently wish Annabel was here, as she's much better at talking to people than I am.

"*Scusi*," I say. "Do you speak English?"

The man shakes his head, and I stumble on. "I'm looking for two friends," I ad-lib. "*Amico. Due amici.* One is very big." I throw my arms wide to indicate Ethan's size. "*Molto grande* and *Americano*. The other is German." I have no idea how to say *German* in Italian. "*Germania*?" I guess and shrug.

We stand staring at each other for a while, and then the man shakes his head. He points back to the main road and waves his hand to the left. "*Apartamenti Rustica*," he says, continuing to wave his hand to the left. "*Due chilometri.*"

Whether he's telling me that Kurt and Ethan are staying in an apartment two kilometers down the road or simply suggesting that it might be a place for me and my dog to try, I have no idea. He might just be trying to get rid of me.

"*Grazie mille,*" I say. The man just grunts, remounts his mower and sets off across the lawn.

I pedal back to the road and turn left.

We pass an olive farm and two more *agriturismo* places before spotting a sign that looks less flashy than all the others: *Apartamenti Rustica*. "If this is the right place," I say to Percy, lowering my voice, "we don't want to just barge in. I think we walk from here." I dismount and push the bicycle into the bushes by the road.

I walk, or, more accurately, hobble, up the dirt road. Percy keeps pace to one side. "I doubt if Annabel's here," I say as much to comfort myself as anything. "Probably just another grumpy Italian."

I don't think I have the strength, physical or mental, to go on much longer. Every muscle in my body aches, I have cuts and scratches everywhere that sting as the sweat runs into them, and my injured left leg is close to seizing up entirely. On top of all that, despite Percy's company, I am becoming steadily more depressed. What began as a pleasant day trip to a cool old town, with the promise of finding tombs full of Etruscan treasure, has turned into a nightmare. I've been chased, I've almost died, and the most important person in the world to me has been kidnapped by some very scary people who are searching for a hoard of stolen Nazi gold. I can't take much more.

Then, through the olive trees, I see the back end of a red ATV sticking out of a rough stone shed.

"There it is, Percy!" I say, instinctively crouching down. I look around. I can't see anyone, but there are other buildings farther up the road. Keeping low and moving from tree to tree, I edge toward the shed. Percy sticks close by me.

The shed is about the same size as the cave on the hillside. The ATV takes up most of the space in it and is definitely the one I saw earlier.

"We've found Annabel," I say to Percy as I slide my iPhone out of my pocket. I'm relieved to see that I have three bars. I scroll to Humphrey Battleford's number and press the Call icon.

"What are you doing here?" A voice behind me makes me jump and drop my phone. Percy barks loudly, and I spin around to see Kurt about ten feet away. He doesn't look happy, and his small black pistol is pointed at my head.

Chapter Eleven

"I thought you were dead," Kurt says, a faint smile curling his thin lips. "You and your annoying friend are causing difficulties."

Percy crouches down low and inches toward Kurt, growling. His teeth are bared, and the hair along his back is standing on end.

Kurt swings his pistol down to point at Percy. "Call off the dog if you want it to live."

"Percy, no," I say. "Come here." I slap my leg. Percy edges back to my side and flops down on his belly. He doesn't take his eyes off Kurt and continues a low grumbling.

"Where is Annabel?" I demand. "What have you done with her? Is she all right?" Despite the pistol pointing back at me, I'm more angry than scared.

"So her name's Annabel. She wouldn't tell us. What are you called?"

"Sam," I say, seeing no point in refusing. "And your name's Brunner."

Kurt looks surprised. "How do you know that?"

"Your grandfather was Max Brunner, a Nazi." It feels good to be one step ahead of Kurt. "He stole the gold you're looking for."

Kurt's smile has gone, replaced by a cold stare that makes me wish I'd kept my mouth shut. "You know too much. How did you find us?"

"I followed you down the hill."

"To rescue your girlfriend. How romantic. Well, you'll join her soon. Does anyone know you're here?"

I hesitate, wondering if it would be better to lie and say yes or admit that I am on my own.

"Your hesitation tells me what I need to know. You are alone."

Percy chooses this time to stand up, stretch as if he didn't have a care in the world, and then trot around behind the stone shed. "Even your dog is deserting you." Kurt says, gloating.

It's hopeless. As I watch Percy leave, I notice, out of the corner of my eye, my iPhone lying in the grass beside a rusty bucket. Maybe if I can get it back, I'll be able to complete my call to Battleford.

I could pretend to trip and fall on it. I'll have to pick my moment. I don't want to startle Kurt while he's holding a gun on me.

My thoughts are interrupted by a fist hitting me square in the back and my feet being swept from beneath me. I fall to the ground, hard. My face is pressed into the dirt, and someone is holding me down. I can see my cell a couple of feet away, but there's no way I can reach it.

I'm hauled roughly to my feet and then I hear that American voice. "Want me to take him up to join the other one?"

To my relief, Kurt lowers the pistol. "Yes. Take him. We'll keep them locked up until we've found the gold. Then we'll decide what to do with them."

Ethan pushes me through the trees toward the main farm buildings. I don't try to talk to him. I just want to get to Annabel and see that she's okay. We veer away from the main building, a stone farmhouse, and head for a small brick building with a high-pitched roof.

"Give me your cell phone," Ethan orders.

"I don't have one," I say.

"Yeah, sure. Everyone has a cell phone. Hand it over."

"Really, I don't have one."

Ethan pats down my pockets and shrugs. I feel relieved that I no longer have the gold bar on me. "What kind of kid doesn't carry a cell phone?" he says, pushing me toward the brick building.

As we get close, I hear a voice. Annabel's. At first I can't make out what she's saying, then all the pressure I've felt since we ran from the tunnel is released. I burst out laughing.

"She's one crazy kid, that," Ethan says. "Won't even tell us her name. Just keeps reciting random numbers nonstop."

"It's Pi," I say as Ethan produces a key and unlocks the padlock on the heavy wooden door.

"What pie?" he asks as he shoves the door open. I ignore his question and push past him into the gloom.

The windows are small and high up, but they let in enough light that I can see Annabel sitting hunched in the far corner. She doesn't look up as the door is opened but keeps counting steadily.

"Annabel," I say.

The counting stops. She looks up. "Sam?" she asks.

"Yeah," I say, my voice choking with emotion. I take a step forward.

In one movement Annabel is on her feet and across the small room, squeezing me in a fierce hug. "I thought you were dead," she sobs into my shoulder.

"Everyone keeps saying that," I say.

"Touching," Ethan sneers as he closes the door behind me.

Annabel pulls back and stares at me hard. "How did you survive going over the cliff?"

"I didn't go over. A big rock stopped me. I crawled back up, and you were gone."

"They took me," Annabel says. "I've been locked up here ever since."

"Reciting Pi," I say.

"Yeah. It really annoys them," she says. "So what happened? How did you find me?" Annabel leads me over to the back wall, and we sit side by side against it. She doesn't let go of my hand.

"I went up to see Pietro," I explain. "He was the only person I could think of who could help. Battleford was there."

"Battleford!"

"Yeah. At first I thought Kurt and Ethan were Battleford's guys, but I don't think he has anything to do with them. Kurt is Max Brunner's grandson."

"The Nazi who hid the gold during the war?"

I nod. "Pietro loaned me his bicycle, and Battleford told me how to get down here. He gave me his cell number and said to call him for help when I found you."

"So let's call him," Annabel says. "They took my cell phone."

"I can't. I dropped my phone when Kurt surprised me. I didn't get a chance to pick it up."

"So we're on our own."

"It looks like it. Battleford sent Percy down with me, but he abandoned me when Kurt showed up. Battleford also said he was going to call the police in Bagnoregio, but it could take them a long time to find us."

We sit silently, thinking about our situation. "What do you think Kurt and Ethan will do to us?" Annabel asks.

"I don't know. Certainly keep us hidden until they find the gold and escape."

"What then?"

I shrug. It worries me how keen Kurt is about waving his pistol around. We sit in silence.

"There's something else I haven't told you," I say finally.

Annabel looks at me, and I lean closer to whisper in her ear. "I found the gold."

"What?" she says loudly.

"Shhhh," I say. "The landslip I fell down uncovered an old cave. There are dozens of gold bars in rotting wooden boxes. I took one up to show Pietro and Battleford."

"If Kurt and Ethan go back up and look around, they'll find it?"

"If no one else does first."

"We have to get out of here and find your cell phone," Annabel says.

"Okay," I agree, "but how? There's no way we can get out of this building short of digging a tunnel."

After a few moments Annabel says, "I have an idea. But you're not going to like it."

"Try me."

"We tell them where the gold is."

"Are you crazy? Even if we do, there's no guarantee they'll let us go once they get it."

"I know," Annabel says. "But if we tell them we can lead them to the gold, that will get us out of here. It'll be difficult for them to keep both of us under control. If I create a diversion, maybe you can run and find your phone and call Battleford."

"That's your plan?" I ask. "We tell them the one thing we don't want them to know and hope one of us manages to run away?"

"Do you have a better plan?"

"No, but—"

I don't have a chance to say anything else. Annabel jumps to her feet and begins hammering on the door. "We know where the gold is!" she yells. "We'll show you if you let us go."

I jump up as well, but my left knee, stiff from sitting, gives way, and all I do is stumble into the wall. Annabel stops banging on the door when we hear the sound of the key being turned in the padlock.

Chapter Twelve

"I am listening," Kurt says. He's standing in the doorway, and I can make out Ethan's bulky form behind him.

"Sam found a chest full of gold bars. We'll show you where if you agree to let us go."

"You are suddenly very talkative," Kurt says. He stares at us both for a long time. "Okay," he says eventually.

He points at me. "You will lead us to the gold." We both take a step toward the door. "But"—Kurt holds up his hand to stop us—"just to make sure there are no tricks, your counting friend will stay here."

Suddenly our weak plan is in ruins. I try to force the issue. "No deal. Either we both go or I won't show you where the gold is."

All my defiance does is make Kurt's pistol appear once more. He points it at Annabel. "Your friend is staying here— either healthy or with a bullet in her leg. Your choice."

I have no doubt that Kurt will do what he threatens. "I'll show you where the gold is," I say quickly.

"Very sensible." Kurt moves aside to let me out. I squeeze past him and limp over to stand beside Ethan. I flex my sore knee while Kurt closes the door and replaces the padlock. Ethan is watching him. This is my chance. I kick out in an attempt to knock Ethan's legs out from under him. There's no power in the blow, and Ethan simply pushes me aside.

Kurt turns to see what's happening, so he doesn't see the large black dog leaping at him. Percy fastens his teeth onto Kurt's right arm, causing him to yell in pain and drop his pistol. Ethan moves to help Kurt, and I take my chance. Ignoring the pain in my knee, I run around the side of the building and into the olive grove.

I have no idea if I'm heading in the right direction. I just keep zigzagging between the gnarled tree trunks. I hear shouts behind me, but I take no notice of them. My breath is coming in ragged gasps and my knee is about to give out when I see the stone shed with the red

ATV sticking out of it. I pause behind a tree. I can see the rusty bucket. I glance back over my shoulder. Kurt and Ethan are a long way back but headed my way. If I can grab my phone and hide, I might have time to call Battleford and tell him where we are.

I dart out to the bucket. I'm so certain I know where my phone is that I am already bending down to grab it when I notice it's not there. Panicking, I look around. There's no cell phone anywhere near the bucket. I kick the bucket over. It bounces away to show a circular patch of dead grass. I don't understand—Kurt and Ethan didn't have time to find the phone. Exhausted and defeated, I slump down on the ground.

Kurt appears from behind an olive tree. He's gasping for breath, and the sleeve of his shirt is torn and blood-stained, but he's retrieved his pistol. Ethan is right behind him.

"Did you hurt Percy?" I ask. "If you harmed him, I'll never tell you where the gold is."

"Very brave," Kurt says between breaths, "but also very stupid. If I did not need you to show me where the gold is, you would already be dead. But that does not mean you cannot be in very much pain when we find the gold."

Kurt nods at Ethan, who steps forward and kicks my injured knee. I scream as jolts of agony run up my leg. He draws back his leg to deliver another blow. I'll tell him anything he wants.

"*Non muoverti. Cadere la pistola e mettere le mani sopra la testa.*"

Two men wearing camouflage pants and T-shirts and carrying automatic weapons appear on either side of the shed. Kurt and Ethan freeze. "*Sbrigati!*" one of the men orders.

Kurt drops his pistol, and he and Ethan raise their hands above their heads.

One of the men moves forward, kicks the pistol to one side and forces the pair to their knees. Using flexible plastic ties, he secures their wrists behind them. Over on the road I see an unmarked jeep roar past in a cloud of dust.

I sit stunned. It's as if I'm in the middle of a movie. None of this is real. Then Humphrey Battleford, with Percy at his heel, steps out from behind the shed. "Quite the adventure," he says casually.

Percy comes over to me, his tail wagging wildly, and licks my cheek. "You were awesome," I say, scratching his ear. "I would never have escaped without your help."

Percy slobbers some more, and I look up at Battleford. "How did you get here?"

"I thought you would be pleased to see me," Battleford says with a smile. "I told you I would call for help, and I have brought some friends."

"What about Annabel?"

"The man in the jeep will not have any trouble with the lock on the door. She will join us shortly."

"But how did you find us?"

Battleford steps forward and hands me my iPhone. "Wonderful things, these," he says. "I received your call, but all I could hear was Percy growling and a German voice saying he thought you were dead. I decided it best to keep quiet."

"That was Kurt. But he didn't say where we were."

"He didn't have to. There's a handy little app that allows one to locate a phone when it's turned on. All I needed to do was run the app, and here we are, the cavalry arriving in the nick of time."

"You can't do this," Ethan says. "I'm an American."

"By coincidence," Battleford says calmly, "so am I. The difference is, I don't go around kidnapping people.

It's an activity the Italian police tend to frown upon, so I suggest you sit quietly for now."

"These don't look like the police," I say, looking at the two men standing over Kurt and Ethan. One of them smiles at me and nods.

"I didn't see the need to involve the authorities at this point," Battleford says. Before I have the chance to ask him more, he looks up. "Ah. I see the lovely Annabel is joining us."

I follow his gaze and see the jeep returning. It stops, and Annabel gets out and runs through the trees. I struggle to my feet, and we embrace. "Are you okay?" I ask.

"I'm fine. You?"

"I'm not dead," I say with a smile.

"Who are these people?" she asks, looking over at the rescuers.

"Friends," Battleford says before I can answer. "But I am being terribly rude. My house is nearby, and I would be honored if you would agree to join me for a late lunch, and perhaps"— Battleford looks over at me—"some attention to those scrapes and bruises."

I don't want to be in further debt to Battleford, but Annabel has no such worries. "We would be delighted to join you for lunch."

Chapter Thirteen

"This is a copy of the rose garden at Malmaison created by Napoleon's wife, Joséphine. Her goal was to collect every rose known. The British sent her roses even though they were at war with France."

"It's beautiful," Annabel says. It turns out that Battleford's house is the towered building we saw along the valley. It's a restored thirteenth-century abbey, and Battleford is giving us a tour. We had a splendid meal of roast boar, and I have had my cuts and scrapes attended to. I even have one of Battleford's walking sticks to take the strain off my injured knee.

Battleford is taking great pleasure in showing off his treasures, and Annabel is being very appreciative. But I'm lagging behind as we stroll through the gardens.

"You are not enjoying yourself?" Battleford turns and asks as we pause beside a life-size bronze statue of a woman in a flowing gown.

"The things in your collection are really cool," I say, "but they make me uncomfortable."

"Because I have stolen them?"

"Yes."

"I admit that many pieces in my collection have been acquired by unconventional means," Battleford says. "That bronze over there." He points to the statue. "That was stolen from a villa buried in the eruption of Vesuvius in 79 AD—but *I* didn't steal it. It was stolen sometime around 1765. I merely purchased it some twenty years ago."

"You should give it back."

Battleford laughs. "To whom? The original owner died two thousand years ago. Do I not have as much right to it as anyone alive today?"

Before I can think of an answer, Annabel joins in. "What do you plan to do with the Nazi gold?"

We both turn and stare at Annabel. She ticks off her fingers. "It's obvious you have it. One, you didn't tell the police we were missing because you would have had to mention the gold. Two, I doubt very much you'd just leave it in an open cave for anyone to find. Three, the back end of the jeep you rescued us in seemed to be riding pretty low."

"Very good," Battleford says with an appreciative smile. "The bullion is indeed in a secure room in the tower of my villa."

"You must give it to the authorities," I blurt out.

"That's the last thing he should do," Annabel says.

"What? I…I…" I stammer.

"Your friend is very clever," Battleford says. "Under Italian law, the gold would be considered treasure, and the authorities would search for the original owners."

"Who were all murdered in the Holocaust," Annabel adds.

"Sadly, you are correct. Of course, there is another possibility. Kurt Brunner may try to claim ownership since it cannot be proven where the gold came from and since it was his grandfather who hid it."

"That can't be allowed to happen!" I shout, horrified at the idea of Kurt and Ethan getting their hands on the gold.

"I agree entirely," Battleford says.

"But you're not entitled to it," I say.

"Actually," Annabel says, "if the owners cannot be traced, then the finder is entitled to half."

"But I am the one who found it," I point out.

"You did," Battleford agrees. "However, if you turn it in to the authorities, I suspect you will be an old man before the case is finished in the courts."

"What can we do?" I ask.

Battleford smiles again. "Fortunately, I have a solution. There were 123 gold bars in the cave. One I gave to Pietro for his museum. The rest is here—122 kilos of gold worth approximately $40,000 US per kilo."

"That's $4,880,000," Annabel says without hesitation.

"Correct," Battleford says. "I propose we each take half. That's $2,440,000 for you as finders, and the same for me as, shall we say, a representative of the authorities."

The chance of suddenly becoming incredibly rich looms in front of me. Images of what I could do and where I could go with that kind of money flash through my brain. But then they're replaced by other images—pale, wide-eyed faces staring out of tiny windows in overpacked cattle cars. Impossibly thin prisoners in striped uniforms standing behind barbed wire. Lines of terrified men, women and children filing past uncaring soldiers in black uniforms. Columns of gray smoke rising from tall chimneys.

"We don't want the money," I say. "People like Max Brunner stole jewelry, wedding rings, even gold teeth, from the millions of people the Nazis murdered at Auschwitz and the other death camps. They melted it down into gold bars so they could use it to escape and live a life of luxury in hiding after the war. I don't want any of it. There's blood mixed in with that gold."

Annabel looks at me with a smile that all the money in the world couldn't buy. She steps over and puts her arm around my shoulder. "Sam's right. We don't want the money. We *should* give the money to the authorities."

"But we don't want Brunner to get any of it," I add.

Battleford looks at us with interest but says nothing.

"I have another proposal," Annabel goes on, squeezing my shoulder. "We don't want the money, and you don't need the money." Battleford nods in acknowledgment. "So why don't we donate the amount the gold is worth to IFAR?"

"IFAR?" I ask.

"The International Foundation for Art Research," Battleford says.

"It's a nonprofit organization," Annabel explains, "that works with other organizations to find lost and stolen artwork and return it to the rightful owners, many of whom are families of those who had art stolen by the Nazis during the war."

"I suppose if I refuse, you will go to the authorities." Battleford rubs his chin thoughtfully. Annabel simply smiles. "Well, then, I think your solution is an admirable one. If it suits you, I shall keep the gold as a historical curio—"

"And an investment, if the value of gold increases," Annabel points out.

"That too," Battleford says. "In return, I shall make a donation of five million dollars to IFAR."

"And ask them to send us a notification when the money arrives," I say.

Battleford laughs. "Never trust a thief."

"What will you do with Kurt and Ethan?" I ask.

"I will treat them like annoying wild animals. My friends will take them far away and drop them off near a town."

"What if they come back?"

"I doubt if they will. With the gold gone, they have no cause to return, and my friends will make it very clear what will happen to them if they don't take the hint."

"Who are your friends?" I ask.

"Probably best if you don't know." Battleford looks at his gold watch. "As always when I run into you two, it has been an interesting day. But now that we have reached an agreement, I will have you driven back to Orvieto before your parents begin to worry.

"But before you go, I have something I think will interest you. And yes, Sam, it was also stolen, but in this case by grave robbers in the seventeenth century. Please come inside and take a quick look at the royal jewelry adorning the mummy of a three-thousand-year-old Etruscan prince."

Chapter Fourteen

"So who won this time?" I ask. Annabel and I are back in the square at Orvieto, sitting in the same café in front of the cathedral, waiting for her parents.

"Hopefully, some of the families who had treasures stolen by the Nazis," she says. "It was strange being on the same side as Battleford for a change."

"Yeah," I agree. "It was also a lot more scary having to deal with Kurt and Ethan."

We sit in silence for a moment, thinking about all our close calls. "You know," I say, "while I was looking for you, I was terrified that they had hurt you badly. I think the pain in my knee helped me. It distracted me from worrying too much about you."

"Oh, thanks," Annabel says with a grin. "What you're saying is that your sore knee was more important than what was happening to me at the hands of two hardened criminals."

"I guess I am," I say, returning the smile.

"But I know what you mean," Annabel goes on. "I was reciting Pi out loud partly to annoy Kurt and Ethan, but also because concentrating on the numbers stopped me thinking about the fact that you were probably dead." Annabel is suddenly close to tears. She reaches across the table and clutches my hand. "I was so scared and lonely in that dark room."

"We must never get split up like that again," I say, returning the squeeze. "Reciting Pi only works once."

"Well," Annabel says, her smile back in place. "It'll help if you watch where you're going and don't go jumping off cliffs."

"I'll try," I say. I look up to see Jack and Pam on their way over to us. "Hey, here come your parents."

"Let's not give them all the details about what happened today," Annabel suggests. "I don't want them to worry."

"Good plan," I say as Pam arrives, kisses us both on the cheek and then waves at a waiter.

Jack joins us. "Do anything exciting today?" he asks.

Born in Scotland, John Wilson is addicted to history and firmly believes that the past must have been just as exciting, confusing and complex to those who lived through it as our world is to us. Most of his thirty-four novels and ten nonfiction books for kids, teens and adults deal with the past. John spends significant portions of his year traveling across the country, telling stories from his books and about their historical background and getting young readers energized and wanting to read and find out more about the past. John lives on Vancouver Island, British Columbia. For more information, visit www.johnwilsonauthor.com.

Titles in the Series
Orca currents

Orca currents

For more information on all the books
in the Orca Currents series, please visit
www.orcabook.com.